How I Was Adopted

· JOANNA COLE ·

How I Was Adopted

Samantha's Story

ILLUSTRATED BY **MAXIE CHAMBLISS**

A MULBERRY PAPERBACK BOOK • NEW YORK

I am deeply grateful to Jan Goldberg for encouraging me to write this book, and for sharing her insights and experience with me. Thanks also to Allison Blank, Bernice Hauser, and Nick and Deborah Dager for reading the manuscript.

Watercolors were used for the full-color illustrations.
The text type is 17-point AGaramond.

www.williammorrow.com
Printed in the United States of America

The Library of Congress has cataloged the Morrow Junior Books edition of *How I Was Adopted* as follows:
Cole, Joanna. How I was adopted: Samantha's story / by Joanna Cole; illustrations by Maxie Chambliss.
p. cm. Summary: A young girl tells the story of how she came to be her parents' child through adoption.
ISBN 0-688-11929-8 (trade). ISBN 0-688-11930-1 (lib. bdg.) [1. Adoption—Fiction.] I. Chambliss, Maxie, ill. II. Title. PZ7.C67346Ho 1995 [E]—dc20 94-42969 CIP AC

1 3 5 7 9 10 8 6 4 2
First Mulberry Edition, 1999
ISBN 0-688-17055-2

A Note to Families

ADOPTION AND LOVE

The story in this book is a happy one. It tells about the eager anticipation of an adoptive couple as they wait to become parents and of the joy they feel when their child finally arrives. It shows a lively little girl, nurtured by parents who love her and enjoy helping her grow up. And it conveys the sense that adoption is just one way of making a family, that the love in an adoptive family is the same as that in any family.

Unlike some other books you may have read, this is not a "problem" book. Instead, it tells the youngest children what adoption is and how it happens and explains honestly that adopted children are not the biological offspring of the people they know as parents. It shows that being a family is about love and spirit, not about blood ties.

I hope that the story in this book will encourage you to talk to your children about their own stories, which cannot come from a book, but only from you. For example, Samantha was adopted through an agency; your child may have had an open adoption. Sam has two parents; yours may be a one-parent family. Sam is a girl; perhaps your child is a boy. Sam is an only child; your child might have siblings, and so on. I hope that reading Samantha's story together will help you and your child talk about your own experience with adoption.

A CHILD'S QUESTIONS

Adopted children often have many questions about themselves and their families. Your child might soon begin asking who her birth parents were and why they relinquished her for adoption; which member of her biological family she resembles; where her birth parents are now and if they think about her; and whether her birth parents are happy and well today. She might want to hear that it was hard for her biological parents to relinquish her for adoption but that they did it out of love, that they lovingly arranged for her to have the things a child needs as she grows up.

A child might want to know why his adoptive parents decided to adopt and to be reassured that they will never change their minds about loving him. He might want to talk about feeling "different" as an adopted child, or about having a sense of loss because he is not the biological child of the people he knows are his parents: you.

Talking with a young child about adoption is a long-term commitment. Certain questions are typical of young children; others usually appear when a child is older, but children of any age may bring up any of these questions. Sometimes a child may ask the same question many times as she grows, incorporating the information each time into her new, more mature view of the world.

Loving parents will welcome any question kids want to ask, but they should avoid piling on material their child is not yet interested in. For example, a very young child may want to tell his adoptive mother how much he wishes he could have grown in her womb, and most of his talk will be about this longing. He may turn later to questions about whose womb he actually grew in.

It is not important how *much* adoptive families talk about adoption. The important thing is to create a loving atmosphere in which children's feelings—both positive and negative—can be shared openly over time. Recent research has shown that one of the most important factors in predicting successful rearing of adopted children is the adoptive parents' positive attitude toward adoption.

Obviously, children's questions are so individual and so varied that parents can't learn stock answers from other people or from books. Only you can decide how to talk with your own child. However, you can get ideas about answering your children's questions by attending group meetings of adoptive parents and by reading articles and books. One book that I found especially helpful in this area is *Talking with Young Children About Adoption,* by Mary Watkins and Susan Fisher (Yale University Press, 1993). Your librarian or bookseller may help you find other titles.

RAISING YOUR ADOPTED CHILD

While the love in an adoptive family is just like the love in any other family, there are some things that make raising adopted children different. Adoptive parents have some extra jobs to do in raising their children, and adopted children have some extra tasks in growing up. One of these is the developmental task of establishing a sense of identity.

Every person develops a concept of who he or she is in relation to the rest of humanity. When my daughter was two, she overheard an introspective adult say half in jest, "I just don't know who I *am* anymore." Rachel said firmly, to the amusement of those around her, "Well, I know who *I* am, because my daddy is Phil and my mommy is Joanna and I am Rachel." Obviously, her toddler identity was bound to her sense of being our child. This identity expands as a child grows to include such things as her biological heritage, her special abilities, her relationship with her peers, her belonging to a certain extended family, a certain ethnic group, a religion, a town, a city, a state, and so on.

For an adopted child, the task of establishing a sense of identity has an added component. Your adopted child sees himself as a child in your family, but he also must integrate his biological heritage and his adoption into his identity. As a parent, you can help. One adoptive mother said of her son, "He has two histories: his history from us of living in Pennsylvania and being the child of Caucasian parents who are a doctor and a graphic artist. He also has his biological heritage, his history of coming from Colombia and having dark hair, eyes, and skin, and of looking forward to visiting Colombia someday."

Part of an adopted child's identity is her relation to you and another part is her biological heritage. Loving parents respect these roots, and that means helping your child learn about the culture of her biological past, answering questions about her biological family in a positive way, and acknowledging that her individual story makes her a special and valuable person.

As Samantha says at the end of this book, "Every girl who was adopted has her own story. Every boy who was adopted has his own story." Every child—adopted or not—deserves to learn about adoption, because chances are that everyone will have a friendship with someone, someday, who either was adopted or is an adoptive parent. And many of today's children may become adoptive parents themselves in the future. I hope Sam's story will be an easy and enjoyable way for children to start finding out about adoption.

Joanna Cole

How I Was Adopted

Hi! My name is Samantha.
You can call me Sam for short.
I live in this apartment house on the second floor.
My room is the one with the pictures in the windows.

I like books, painting,
guinea pigs, and the color red.
Can you see what else I like?

I *love* my mommy and daddy, and they love me.
They play with me.

They take care of me.
And they give me lots of hugs and kisses!

Mommy told me that I was adopted.
Were you adopted, too?

Daddy told me how old I was when I was adopted:
I was one week old!
Do you know how old you were when you were adopted?

Before I was adopted, I was born.
Daddy and Mommy told me how babies are born.
They said that every baby grows
in a special place inside a woman's body.
That place is called her uterus.

When a baby is ready to be born,
the woman's uterus squeezes and squeezes,
and the baby comes out into the world!

Many children stay with the woman
who gave birth to them.
Some children do not.
Some children need to be adopted,
the way Mommy and Daddy adopted me.

I did not grow inside Mommy's uterus.
I grew in another woman's uterus.
Some special things about me
were there when I was born—
my blue eyes,
my curly hair,
the freckle on my knee,
and my being a girl!

SAM
SAM

I ♥ DAD
MOM
DAD
SAM

The rest of me—
what I know,
how I talk,
the jokes I like,
the things I can do—
came from just being me
and growing up in my family.

One day I asked Daddy and Mommy how I was adopted.
They told me the story.

First, they showed me pictures of themselves
before they had me.
They told me how they met each other.
They told me how they started to love each other.

"We had so much love," said Mommy.
"We wanted to share it with a child
and be a family," said Daddy.

Daddy and Mommy wanted to adopt a child,
so they asked an adoption counselor to help them find one.
"A long time went by," said Mommy.
"It was hard to wait," said Daddy.

“Then one day the phone rang,” said Mommy.
“It was the adoption counselor.
She said there was a child for us.

Imagine how excited we were!”

Mommy and Daddy went to meet the counselor.
She put a baby in Mommy's arms.
Guess who that baby was.
It was me—Samantha!

“You were so cute,” said Mommy.
“We loved to hold you.”
“You were so hungry.
We loved to feed you,” said Daddy.

“You were so sleepy. We took you home
and put you in a little crib.
We covered you up to keep you warm,” said Mommy.

"Our friends and relatives came to welcome you," said Daddy.
"We took lots of pictures of you," said Mommy.

"Soon you started smiling and reaching,
and sitting and crawling,

and walking and talking,
and playing with toys,

and making friends,
and looking at books!

You gave us lots of hugs and kisses!"

I love to hear Mommy and Daddy tell about how I was adopted.
It's my very own story.
Every girl who was adopted has her own story.
Every boy who was adopted has his own story.

Do you know the story of how *you* were adopted?